W9-BOA-227

RYE FREE READING ROOM

For Megan, Charlie,
Lucy and George –
and thank you to Grandpa.

First American edition published in 2011 by Andersen Press USA,
an imprint of Andersen Press Ltd.
www.andersenpressusa.com

First published in Great Britain in 2010
by Andersen Press Ltd.,
20 Vauxhall Bridge Road, London SW1V 2SA.
Published in Australia by Random House Australia Pty.,
Level 3, 100 Pacific Highway, North Sydney, NSW 2060.
Copyright © Jo Hodgkinson, 2010
Jacket illustrations copyright © Jo Hodgkinson, 2010

The author and the artist assert the moral right to be identified as author and
artist of this work. All rights reserved. No part of this book may be reproduced,
stored in a retrieval system, or transmitted in any form or by any means—
electronic, mechanical, photocopying, recording, or otherwise—without the
prior written permission of Andersen Press Ltd., except for the inclusion
of brief quotations in an acknowledged review.

Distributed in the United States and Canada by
Lerner Publishing Group, Inc.
241 First Avenue North
Minneapolis, MN 55401 U.S.A.
www.lernerbooks.com

Color separated in Switzerland by Photolitho AG, Zürich.
Printed and bound in Singapore by Tien Wah Press.

Library Cataloging-in-Publication Data available.
ISBN: 978-0-7613-7487-9

1 - TWP - 9/8/10
This book has been printed on acid-free paper.

JO HODGKINSON

THE TALENT SHOW

ANDERSEN PRESS USA

A sign stopped four friends in their tracks.
The news sent shivers down their backs.

A small red bird who'd seen it too
flew down to get a better view.
He quietly said, "I'd like a go
to try and win this Talent Show."

The four friends laughed. "Don't be absurd!
You're much too small. You're just a bird."

With that, the friends went on their way
to practice for this special day.

At home they practiced
day and night
to get their tunes to
sound just right.

They felt the rhythm,
tapped their feet
until they found a steady beat.

The Bear and Lion, Snake and Croc
played tunes that made the whole house ROCK.

This band could play. This band could move.

This band had really found its groove.

But all of a sudden,
the drums went

BOOM!

This wasn't a beat
to match the tune.

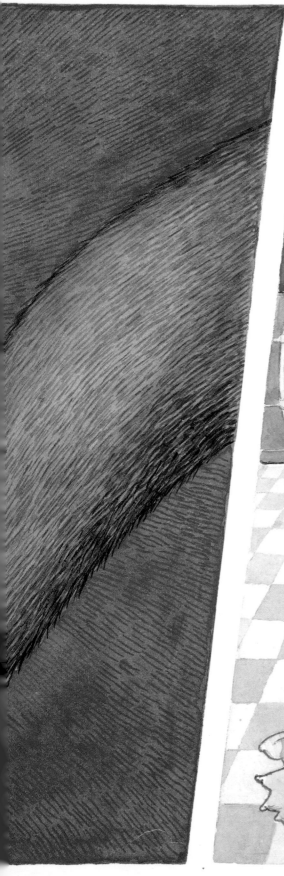

Bear stood up and
scratched his head,
looked quite serious,
sighed, and said,

"If we want to
win this thing,
one of the band
will have to sing."

So everybody took a turn
to sing a song that they had learned.

But the only sounds that
they could make
were GRR, SNAP, GROWL
and HISS of Snake.

This came as quite a big surprise.
"I know," said Croc, "let's advertise!"
They hung a sign up on the tree,
so singers passing by might see.

SINGER
WANTED

auditions
today

This way

Well not much time
had passed before
they heard a knock
at their front door.

As Bear looked out
onto the street,
he heard a voice
down by his feet.

"I saw the sign so down I flew.

I've come to have an interview."

Bear growled,
"There's nothing left to say.
You're much too small.

Now GO AWAY!"

Singers came from all around.

But no one had that missing sound. With no hope left, what would they do?
The band sat down to think things through. When suddenly they got a shock . . .

a loud, resounding KNOCK KNOCK KNOCK!

They looked and
saw an eerie sight:
a stranger standing
in the night.

His coat was long,
his glasses black,
and on his head
he wore a hat.

He said, "I've come
to help you win
this Talent Show.
Can I come in?"

He sang the most amazing songs.

The band began to play along.

They knew this was
the missing sound.

At last, their singer
had been found.

But as he sang and danced around, the stranger's coat fell to the ground.

And in their presence now, they saw
the bird they'd laughed at twice before.

"Red Bird, will you forgive us, please?
We realize we were wrong to tease."

Bird said, "You really were unwise
to simply judge me by my size.
But now I see you understand
and I'd be glad to join your band."

The next day at the Talent Show,
the five were waiting for their go.

But as they stepped into the light . . .
the small red bird was filled with fright.

He felt so small and all alone.
He thought about his treetop home.
He wished that he could fly away.
But then his friends began to play . . .

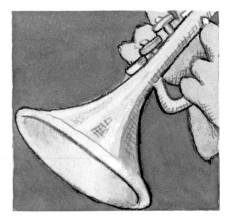

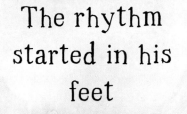

The rhythm started in his feet

and traveled quickly to his beak.

The sound made by that little bird was quite the best the crowd had heard.

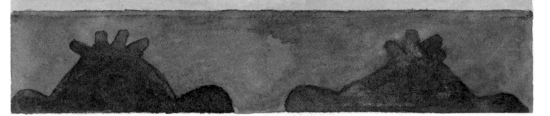

The crowd got up, they danced and swayed
to every tune the great band played.

And as the crowd began to cheer,
Bird saw he had no need to fear.
The judges gave the band the prize.
They judged on talent, not on size.

FICTION HODGKINS ON
Hodgkinson, Jo.
The talent show.
03/05/2011
LC 2/11/20   45X   R 12/20

DO NOT DISCARD
CHILDRENS CORE
COLLECTION

RYE FREE READING ROOM
1061 BOSTON POST RD.
RYE NY 10580
914—967—0480